Sunny Pines

Sunny Pines

Ray Garton
Bev Vincent
Kealan Patrick Burke
Glen Krisch

CEMETERY DANCE PUBLICATIONS

❖ *Baltimore* ❖

2022

Cemetery Dance Publications
132B Industry Lane, Unit #7
Forest Hill, MD 21050
www.cemeterydance.com

The characters and events in this book are fictitious.
Any similarity to real persons, living or dead,
is coincidental and not intended by the authors.

Trade Paperback Edition

ISBN:
978-1-58767-852-3

Cover Artwork and Design © 2022 by Alan M. Clark
Cover and Interior Design © 2022 by Desert Isle Design, LLC

This novella was written as a collaborative effort between the four authors. The first author wrote the first section and handed the story off to the second author for the second section, etc. Each author wrote one section, and the name in bold at the top of a page is the author who wrote that section. You may notice that Glen Krisch undertook the yeoman's work of wrapping up the story to a proper conclusion, and for his efforts we are all grateful!

One

Conner had not seen his old friend Miguel in more than twenty years, and it took them a while to get through all the hugging and laughing and mutual compliments. Their reunion took place at dusk in the parking lot of the 7-Eleven across the street from the trailer park where they had grown up together.

After spending the day driving there from Los Angeles—it was a good twelve-hour drive from one end of California to the other—Conner wanted a cup of coffee, so they went inside. It was a dizzying experience. They used to meet friends in that parking lot when they were kids, then go into the store to drop their quarters into the video games lined up in the front while they drank their Slurpees and ate their potato chips and M&Ms and Red Vines, or whatever they could afford with the change they'd fished out of their couches or pilfered from their parents. Conner had been fifteen the last time he'd entered the store, and it didn't look much different now than it had then. A little run-down and tired, maybe. The video games were gone and the prices were much higher.

They took coffee and donuts back to the parking lot, stood between their cars, and did a little catching up. Miguel still lived in town, had a wife and two daughters, and owned a busy auto shop. Conner was an illustrator currently working on a modestly popular werewolf comic book. As the day's light gave way to darkness, the glow from the store's glass front moved farther out into the parking lot, as if reaching for them.

"Have you seen Jelica yet?" Conner said.

"No. She should be here soon."

"When did you last see her?"

"Same time you did. That Christmas we were all together. What was it, twenty… *two* years ago? Something like that."

Conner finished his cruller and tossed the napkin through the open window of his car to avoid littering. "I'm sorry we lost touch. All three of us."

"It happens. People grow up, grow apart, and have separate lives." He grinned. "We sure had some fun times when we were together, though, didn't we?"

Conner smiled, but he sounded melancholy when he said, "We did."

In spite of everything, he added silently.

Miguel's single mother had some serious mental problems and had self-medicated with alcohol and drugs, eventually self-medicating herself into an early grave. While she was alive, her wild mood swings and violent behavior had made Miguel—they called him Miggy back then—a frightened, nervous wreck. Conner was happy to see that he'd grown into a calm, quiet man with an easy smile.

Conner's mother, Trudy, did everything she could, including selling drugs and herself, to support her abusive, drug-addicted husband, Jerry, who hated Conner and used to enjoy beating him severely. Conner's real dad was still alive then, but in prison for manslaughter after killing another occupant of Sunny Pines in a drunken fight. Trudy was rarely home because she usually held down two jobs just to keep them in that beaten-up old trailer they called home. Jerry was home most of the time because he didn't work and had nowhere to go. Conner had chosen to spend as much time as possible away from the trailer and with his friends.

Anjelica Palmer had endured much worse than either of them. Her mother Phyllis shuffled from one waitress job to the next, never holding them for long. She supplemented her income with the generosity of her male friends, none of whom stayed around very long, but most of whom at least left a tip. The best and worst part of growing up for Anjelica was having three siblings. But over time, and under the pressures exerted by her financial benefactors, Phyllis peeled away her offspring until none but Angelica remained.

Jelica, the youngest, had been born with hypoplasia of the vocal cords and had never been able to speak. Anyone who knew Phyllis was not surprised given the fact that she remained quite drunk throughout all of her pregnancies. If anything, people were surprised that her babies hadn't been born with much worse afflictions.

Conner remembered the noises that used to come from Jelica's trailer: loud music, hysterical laughter, the harsh, slurred cries of Phyllis rutting with one of her men, and sometimes, far too often, the sound of Jelica's sister Marilyn screaming in fear or pain. One day, when she was eleven, Jelica woke up to see Marilyn's bed made, as if she hadn't slept there, as if she no longer existed. The Palmer siblings were down to one, and Jelica was left to fend for herself.

Jelica, who had no voice and could not scream. But Conner and Miggy heard her, anyway, and shared her fear and pain. They heard her in the only place where Jelica did have a voice: their minds. In addition to being the only people who called her Jelica, Conner and Miggy were the only people with whom she could communicate telepathically besides her Great Aunt Pia, who had died a number of years before she moved to the 'Pines. She had worried that she'd never have that kind of relationship again with anyone until she discovered that it worked with her two friends.

Conner knew that he and Miggy and Jelica were not the only children in the mobile home park to have difficult lives. No one at Sunny Pines was happy. The nights were filled with angry shouting, screaming, the sounds of shattering glass, and occasional gunfire. The police made frequent visits and were usually quite open about how much they hated having to answer calls there.

Sunny Pines

All of that had happened directly across the street from where Conner and Miguel now stood.

Conner had avoided looking in that direction as he talked with Miguel.

"Have you been in touch with her?" Conner said.

"Not until I got the email yesterday."

"Does she still live here?"

"I don't know where she lives. Around here somewhere, I'm guessing, because she knew about the fire right away."

"Yeah, but... well, you know Jelica. Just because she knew about the fire right away doesn't mean anyone told her, and it doesn't mean she was anywhere near here."

"I wonder if that's still true," Miguel said quietly, almost whispering. He turned his head to look across the street. "That was a long time ago. Sometimes people... outgrow things."

"I don't think that's something you outgrow. Besides, she told us this was going to happen years ago."

Miguel nodded, then looked at him and smiled. "The elephant in the room, right?"

"Yeah, I guess so. That's why she wanted us to meet. It must be." Then, after a moment: "Don't you think?"

Miguel nodded as he turned to look across the street again. "What was it she said again? Something about the ground."

"Yeah. She said the ground was bad, and that's why everybody in Sunny Pines was miserable."

Conner finally turned and looked in the direction of the trailer park. There was nothing but darkness across the street beyond the seven-foot cinderblock wall that surrounded Sunny Pines. Normally, there would be a glow rising above that wall from the trailers and tall lights in the park. A light had always shone above the big sign in front illuminating the name of the park in big black letters, but now, even the sign was swallowed up by the darkness. There seemed to be nothing there but the wall, as if the place where Conner and Miguel had grown up had never been.

10

"How many died in the fire?" Conner said.

"Six people killed, about twenty injured. Some may still die. Everything within the walls of Sunny Pines burned. Branches that hung over the fence from trees outside the park burned, but the trees they were attached to were left standing. Nothing burned beyond the walls."

Conner felt a sudden shudder of unreasonable fear move through him. He tried to cover it up by finishing off his coffee, crushing the cup in his hand, and tossing it into his car.

He looked up at the night sky but it was overcast and no stars were visible. "We were watching the stars come out, weren't we?"

Miguel nodded. "It was a clear Fall night. We were lying on the ground near the swing set, staring up at the sky."

They talked while they watched the stars slowly wink into existence in the darkening sky, but not aloud. About nothing important, just small talk. Jelica lay between Conner and Miggy in the small Sunny Pines playground, among the rusting old swing set and dented slide. As the night closed in, Conner noticed that Jelica had become quiet. Her silence was followed by a dark feeling, as dark as the sky, that crept through him and steadily grew. It was a frightening, choking feeling of horror and despair. He sat up with a jerk and looked down at Jelica.

The moonlight fell on her in a pale, powdery blue. Surrounded by her red hair, the freckled face that usually held a smile for everyone, even in the worst of conditions, looked horrified. Her eyes were clenched shut and the corners of her mouth were drawn back to their limit in an expression made up of terror and pain as she closed her hands around fistfuls of gravel. She breathed increasingly faster until she was almost panting like a dog.

Miggy sat up too, saying, "Whassamatter?"

"Jelica!" Conner shouted, clutching her forearm. "Jelica, what do we do?"

Her body was so rigid that it trembled all over with tension and she gave no sign that she heard him or was aware of their presence. Both boys stared at her in open-mouthed horror, frozen in place on each side of her, until her body suddenly fell limp and still. Her breathing slowed, her face relaxed, and her fists loosened. She lay still for a moment, then, eyes wide and fearful, she frantically scrambled to her feet and looked around as if confused.

"What's wrong?" Conner said as he and Miggy stood, too.

She was pale and shaken, afraid of something, as she looked down at her feet.

When she said nothing for a moment, the boys looked down, too. They saw only the gravel on the ground.

It's there, in the ground, she said in their minds.

Connor looked down again, saw nothing, and replied, "What's in the ground?"

She slowly turned around and looked at all the mobile homes that surrounded them, then her eyes moved back and forth between the boys as she told them, *Everything that's wrong with this place, with the people. It's in the ground. It... it maybe is the ground.*

Their look of bafflement was all the response she needed.

Nobody's happy here, she said. *All the drugs and liquor and the beatings... so much bad stuff. And it's all in this one small trailer park. But it's not the people. They're not bad, not really, not inside. It's the place. The ground. It's in the ground.*

"But what is it?" Miggy said.

Jelica slowly turned her head from side to side. *I don't know. I don't think I want to know because it's bad. Real bad.* She hugged herself as if cold when she added, *I don't even want to be here anymore. It's not safe. And someday...*

She left the statement unfinished, hanging open in the air between them.

"Someday what?" Conner said.

Well, it's not going to stay in the ground forever. Someday, it'll come up and just... swallow all of us. All of us and maybe... everything.

Twenty-eight years had passed since that strange night. Conner wondered what she had been doing, what kind of life she'd led, and if he would be able to recognize her if he saw her on the street. He was eager to see her, but not under those circumstances. Not at Sunny Pines.

"She really wants us to go *in* there?" Conner said as he and Miggy stared across the street into the dark.

"That's what the email said."

"What if we can't get in?"

"We can. I checked it out this afternoon. They've got it blocked off, but it'll be no problem getting in there on foot."

Conner's disappointment was in his sigh. "The thing is... I don't know if I *want* to go in there."

He imagined the blackened remains of the trailer park that awaited them, the twisted, burnt skeletons of melted mobile homes in which people had been burned alive. The images in his mind were like something out of an H.P. Lovecraft story.

We haven't seen each other in all these years and you're gonna chicken out on me? Jelica's voice asked in Conner's head.

Conner and Miguel flinched and looked at each other with surprise. Miguel had received it, too. They looked around to find her as a blue Volkswagen Beetle drove into the 7-Eleven parking lot. It pulled into the slot beside Conner's car. The door opened and Jelica smiled at them as she came out of the car, closed the door, and hurried to them with her arms wide.

The best friends I ever had! The words filled Conner with a warm melancholy as she hugged both of them at once. When she pulled away, Conner realized that all three of them had tears in their eyes.

Two

Conner and Miguel wiped their eyes and stood back to drink their old friend in. Jelica's freckles had faded, mostly, but her red hair still blazed. Strands of gray threaded through it now, and there were creases around her eyes and the corners of her mouth, but all in all it looked like the years had been kind to her.

"Jelica. So great to see you," Conner said. "Where are you living these days?"

Her answer appeared inside his head, but it was much more than words. He understood what she was saying—*On a vineyard near Healdsburg*—but he also saw the place, as if he were watching a video from a camera-mounted drone. The farmland stretched for what looked like miles, beside a meandering river. The vineyard appeared prosperous, with acres of hardy vines, modern equipment and a number of well-tended buildings.

But he saw something else, too. A dark cloud that expanded to reveal a husband and two children, a boy and a girl. An accident on a narrow, winding, hilly road through the redwoods. Conner saw the transport that rounded a corner too wide, crowding the vehicle containing Jelica and her family off the edge of an embankment. He was with her in the hospital when the doctors broke the news about the others. Experienced briefly her long and painful recuperation.

Sunny Pines

It took only a few seconds, but it was all there—everything important about her life, and how much of it had been taken from her three years ago. Conner glanced at Miguel. Based on the stunned look on his friend's face, he assumed Miguel had gotten the message, too. Conner wondered how much of the intervening decades she was able to read from his or Miguel's mind.

Don't look so sad, Jelica projected. *We were happy for a lot of years. Happiest time of my life.*

They had all come from the same place and had survived. Made something of themselves. Tragedies happened to everyone, even those who'd had happy childhoods, Conner knew. There was no reason to connect what had occurred to Jelica's family to Sunny Pines.

And yet, he had perceived darkness, and he couldn't help looking across the street to the place where they had once played together and fended off the worst life had to throw at them. Or so they'd thought at the time.

For years, Conner had struggled to rise above his turbulent and violent upbringing, but it kept coming back. At first in dreams and then, later, in his illustrations, which had garnered him some notice, a few minor awards and the most recent gig. People often asked him about the darkness within his work. Bleakness was to be expected—he was drawing werewolves gleefully eviscerating people, after all—but there was something else, a shadow that lurked at the edges. Now, standing across from the trailer park, he knew the source of that shadow. *Sunny Pines*, he mused. *Ever a misnomer.*

They spent a few minutes catching up, but it didn't take long, thanks to Jelica's abilities. "You've gotten so much stronger," Miguel said. "I can see it all in my mind."

Jelica nodded. *But only with you two,* she said. *It doesn't work with anyone else. It's wonderful to be able to communicate freely again, after all these years.*

"It didn't work with your husband?"

She shook her head. *My kids, either, and let me tell you there were times when I wished I could read their minds.*

They were quiet for a while, still staring in the direction of Sunny Pines. Conner wondered what the ruined land within had in store for them. What would be its next surprise? He could sense power waiting to burst free and unleash… something terrible. He noticed that the light from the convenience store window had reached the edge of the road, but it wasn't likely to go much farther, he thought. Whatever lurked inside those scorched cinderblock walls would devour it.

"Why do you think it erupted now?" Miguel asked.

It's ready, Jelica said.

"For what?" Conner asked, but Jelica merely shrugged, and no visions came.

"I overhear things at the shop," Miguel said. "Someone said today that a developer wants to snap up the property. He plans to build apartments or condos or something. People were speculating that the fire was awfully convenient for him."

Jelica's face paled. *We have to fix this now, while we have the chance. Before anyone does something with the land. Remember what went on around us? All the time? Imagine if even more people lived here, piled on top of one another.*

Conner pictured a nuclear explosion, complete with mushroom cloud. He wasn't sure if it came from his own imagination or from Jelica's.

"Do we really have to go back in there?" Miguel asked.

Jelica nodded. *Yeah, Miggy. We do.*

He smiled a bit, hearing his old nickname. "Now? In the dark?"

She nodded again.

"But what can we do? We're just three people—a mechanic, a guy who draws comics, and a woman who makes wine?"

"Graphic novels, I'll have you know," Conner said. The serious look on his face belied his light tone.

Jelica nodded toward her car. *I came equipped. I've done my homework over the years. Sunny Pines has never been out of my thoughts for very long.*

It seemed as natural as anything, communicating with her like this. For the longest time, Conner had convinced himself that their special relationship was part of a childhood fantasy he'd created to help survive the abuse and the psychological torment to which he'd been subjected. He remembered their long, wordless conversations clearly—so clearly that he'd become certain that they were a fabrication. After all, how could it be otherwise? Mind reading and telepathy belonged in fiction— or in the graphic novels he illustrated. And, yet, here they were again, reading Jelica's thoughts and seeing her memories. Communicating without words.

They were silent for a moment as they contemplated the place where they had grown up, despite every adult in their lives' best efforts to destroy them. It seemed appropriate that the place had finally gone up in flames. *Two decades too late,* Conner mused.

Jelica nodded.

"So, what's the plan?" Miguel asked. "My wife's expecting me home sometime tonight."

You may be a little late. Jelica had a wry smile on her face. *I'd like to meet her.*

Conner hoped they'd be able to meet anyone after this night was over. He had an idea that Jelica's plan was dangerous. He believed her when she'd said that something lurked in the earth—it was the main reason why he'd moved so far away. Being back here, flooded with terrible childhood memories, it was so easy to believe in malevolent ground again.

"So, what exactly are we up against?" Miguel asked as Jelica popped the trunk on her Beetle.

Evil, Jelica said and handed Miguel a backpack. *Pure and simple.*

"How do you know?"

Do you guys trust me? she said as she handed another backpack to Conner.

"Of course we do, right Bro?" Miguel looked to Conner.

"Yeah, sure we do. Just one question: what's in the packs?" He lifted the pack she'd handed him. It was relatively light, weighing no more than ten pounds. Miguel's pack looked much heavier. He even grunted as he shouldered it.

Equipment, she said. She shouldered her own pack and shut the trunk. *I'll explain it all when we get inside.*

———————

I left here not long after the last time we saw each other. As soon as I had saved enough money to buy a cheap set of wheels and get a place to stay, I beat it the hell out of here. Never looked back. The only thing I regretted leaving behind was you two. My best friends, until I met my husband, Gary.

I headed out into the countryside. Always dreamed of living on a farm. Found a winery looking for seasonal help and hired on. Until then, I didn't realize life could be so carefree and happy. The work was hard, but I loved every second of it.

Conner and Miguel watched Jelica toiling in the fields, shoring up vines, taking care of animals, helping around the house, participating in the harvest. She always seemed to have a smile on her face.

But I never stopped thinking about Sunny Pines.

"Your mother was still here?" Conner asked.

Yes, but that didn't matter. She didn't look after my sister and me. And she gave my brothers up for adoption long before I even left, remember? I didn't hate her, not really, but once I was gone I didn't think about her much. I thought about the ground here, though. A lot. In my spare time, I went to the library and started doing research.

"Was your mother here when the…?" Conner trailed off, but indicated the burned wreckage on the other side of the road.

Jelica shook her head. *She died a long time ago. Most of the people we knew when we were kids are gone. Residents of Sunny Pines lived short, brutal lives. What about your mom? And that nasty man she married?*

"Jerry. Nope. Both long gone. And good riddance to him."

"Guess we're the lucky ones," Miguel said.

Jelica nodded and continued her story. *How much high school history do you remember? Remember the missions built by the Franciscans in the late 18th Century? They wanted to convert the natives to Catholicism and educate them, so they created this network of missions along the Pacific coast, as far north as Sonoma.*

19

Sunny Pines

Conner and Miguel nodded.

What the history books don't say, because there are no written records, is that the Spanish weren't the first outsiders who attempted to colonize the area. The natives have an oral tradition about settlers who arrived from the sea over a hundred years before that. No one knows where they really came from. Some people believe they weren't human at all, that when the elders say "from the sea" they actually mean that they came from somewhere outside of the known realm. Maybe even from another universe, dimension, or from outer space.

It's clear from the legends that these people were very powerful. There weren't many of them, but they overthrew every settlement and every tribe they encountered.

Rumors of their progress spread up and down the coast, but even with advanced warning, no village was able to fend them off. Any place they conquered, no crops grew for generations. Certain patches of earth in particular were known among the natives as black spots, dead sections of land their people were not allowed to live near. There are stories of fierce battles within tribes who rebuilt villages in those regions. Hatred and suspicion grew deep, a kind of paranoia that was only alleviated once everyone there had died or moved on to greener pastures.

Jelica's narrative filled their minds, a motion picture that played out her words like an historical re-enactment. Conner and Miguel had no idea how she could create such a vivid depiction of something she hadn't witnessed first-hand, but when it came to their childhood friend, they had far more questions than answers. It almost didn't do to probe too deeply.

Just as quickly and mysteriously as they arrived, the invaders vanished. Over the following decades and centuries, shamans tended to the black spots they left behind and were able to heal most of them—to make them livable and arable once more, although many tribes continued to mistrust those areas and still avoid them to this day. There was at least one, though, that they were never able to rid of its darkness. White men took over the land around it and kept the natives at bay. There has always been a settlement of some sort near there, and it has always been a source of violence and misery.

"Sunny Pines," Conner said. "I hate that name. Where did you learn all of this?"

When he was drinking—which was most of the time—my grandfather used to call my grandmother a squaw. Out of curiosity, I had my ancestral DNA tested a few years ago, and the results confirmed that I have some native blood. Enough to satisfy me that my grandmother and her sister—my Great Aunt Pia—were Native American. Maybe that explains how I was able to communicate with Pia.

"But what about us? I don't have any Indians in my family tree."

Maybe it has something to do with spending so much time here. Jelica shrugged, and Conner was struck, not for the first time, by how beautiful she had become. Would she be able to read that thought, he wondered. She didn't react, but part of him hoped so.

It took a long time, and for years I thought I'd never get to the bottom of the mystery, but I eventually discovered that Pia and her sister were from the Coast Miwok tribe. I then earned the trust of the elders of one of the bands who live at Middletown Rancheria. That's where I met Gary. He's half Pomo. Well, he was.

She shook off a momentary fugue. *He owned the vineyard where I live now, and he hired a lot of people from the Rancheria, so he was well-liked there. That gave me the inside track, and they told me all these stories, often around a campfire at night, with a sky full of stars above us. It was magical. They listened to my story about Sunny Pines and revealed to me the legends of the black spots and the rituals the shamans performed to purify them. I was a woman with only a quarter native blood, so it was a great honor to be entrusted with their secrets and their rites.*

"So, what are we going to do?"

What the shamans were never able to do. Purify the land. Cleanse Sunny Pines.

Three

"I hate to point out the obvious," Conner said. "But we're not shamans. And if what you're saying is true then even the actual bona fide ones weren't able to purify those spots in the earth. How exactly is it that you think we're going to fare any better than they did against these ghosts or whatever they are?"

They're not ghosts, Jelica told him. *I wish they were.*

"Really?" Miguel chimed in. "Because I don't."

If I tell you, you won't come with me.

"Considering what you're asking us to do, don't you think you should tell us everything up front?" Miguel said.

Conner agreed, but hesitated to voice the concern. Besides, chances were Jelica had already detected it, if not from his mind, then certainly from the tension apparent in his bones. He had never considered himself a coward. No, Jerry had done a good job beating any trace of that out of him the one day he'd come home from school with a bloody nose and someone else's phlegm drying on his shirt. Despite the frequent abuse, it had nevertheless had the intended effect, and he'd lived the rest of his life protected by a hardened shell few adversities or adversaries had managed to penetrate. It had served him well, perhaps a little too well, and often he found himself wondering what that armor had cost him. He had never managed to maintain a relationship for more than a year, with friends or lovers. All he had left were acquaintances, the connection he'd forged out of necessity and loneliness with Miguel, and the decades-long crush on the girl standing before him now.

Even after twenty-two years, they were all he had left. That loyalty had brought him here against his better judgment and despite the conviction that Jelica would not show and that if she did, she would inadvertently lead them all back where they had no business going, back to a place they'd been lucky enough to escape the first time.

Sunny fucking Pines, a stain on his rearview.

No, he had outgrown fear, but goddamnit he was afraid now, and didn't need to be a mind-reader to know Miguel was too. If Jelica shared their fear, she hid it well.

"What are they if not ghosts?" he asked, if only to keep her from reading too clearly what had been on his mind. It had been a problem more than once when they were young, especially when he'd caught himself looking at her long pale legs or the nubs of her budding breasts through her hand-me-down blouse and his thoughts had run away from him before he could think to catch them. As a result he had learned early to focus his mind's eye on something less salacious lest she expose him. Like how the Raiders were doing, or how it would look if he used his steel bat to bash Jerry's fucking brains in.

I don't know, Jelica admitted. *I don't think anyone does.*

"And you think if they're here they're just going to let us waltz in and slam shut the hellhole they opened?" He stepped close and gently put his hands on Jelica's shoulders. "Look, I'm with you all the way. Both of us are, right Miggy?"

Miguel nodded, but looked equally unsure. Conner understood why. Of them all, he had the most to lose. Neither Conner nor Jelica had anyone left who cared about them. Miguel still had a family waiting for him at home.

"You tell us what to do and we'll do it," Conner continued. "I just want you to be sure you know what we're walking into, because I love you, both of you, and I don't want anyone getting hurt… or worse."

Neither do I, Jelica told him, her eyes searching his, looking for something he was abruptly terrified to think might not be there: empathy. *But if we don't do this, those condos go up and then people* will *get hurt. Look behind you, Conner. Six people dead while they slept, two of them children. Eight more are in critical condition. This is not a pattern that has an ending unless* we end it.

"How do we know it'll work?" Miguel asked, nervously picking at the skin around the fingernail on his oil-stained thumb.

Jelica looked at him. *Even if it doesn't, we have to at least* try, *don't we?* She averted her gaze from both of them then in favor of studying a jagged crack in the asphalt at her feet. *I know I do, at least, because I knew this would happen. I let those people die.*

"No," Conner said, squeezing her shoulders. "No you didn't. Don't say that. You were just a kid. We all were. You couldn't have known—"

But I did know.

"Listen to me. You *don't* get to say that. Know why? Because if you take the blame, then we all have to, and I have enough darkness in my life without adding the guilt of six dead people on top of it."

Then come with me and let's make sure the darkness here ends with us, tonight, so we don't all go our separate ways and spend the next who-knows-how-many years waiting to hear about another tragedy we could have prevented, or watching the news waiting for it. Will you be able to live with that? I know I can't.

Conner dropped his hands from her shoulders, looked at Miguel, and then back into the face of the woman he realized in that moment he had never stopped loving. He knew then that she was right, and that even if any doubts remained and the fear was enough to tie his insides in knots, he would follow her wherever she asked him to go.

"Okay," he said.

Miguel exhaled heavily and nodded. "Yeah, okay."

Whatever happened next, the bond that was forged between them standing there in the 7-Eleven parking lot was stronger than it had ever been before. And just maybe, Conner thought, when it came down to it and they found themselves face to face with the evil beyond those walls, that would be the thing that made all the difference.

"So how do we get in?"

"It's blocked off, but not very well," Miguel said.

I imagine the effort to seal it off would have been half-hearted, Jelica added as they left the parking lot and crossed the street. *Worrying about people breaking into a razed trailer park wouldn't be a major concern. I'm guessing there's not much left to steal or vandalize.*

To Conner, the air seemed to grow colder the closer they got to the cinderblock wall, though that might just have been his body acclimating. The parking lot blacktop would have retained the day's heat. *Sure, that's it,* he told himself, and realized Jelica was rubbing her arms. Miguel had his hands buried in his pockets, his body tight. Whatever the cause of the sudden drop in temperature, natural or preternatural, it was clear they all felt it.

"Do you think it… the thing in there… the ground… did anything to the people trying to help?" Conner asked.

I don't know, Jelica replied, *but I suspect it left them alone. It probably felt they were too trivial to bother with. I think it prefers a larger canvas, like, say, a community to corrupt.*

"Good," Conner said. "Let's hope it feels we're too trivial to bother with too."

Jelica looked at him. *I'd like to say I think that'll be the case, but…*

"But it knows we're coming," Conner finished for her. "And why we're here, right?"

She nodded once, and then abruptly stopped, her face raised to the cinderblock wall, eyes wide. Her hand found Conner's forearm and squeezed hard, but any vestige of pleasure he might have drawn from the contact was obliterated by the look on her face.

Look, she said.

He didn't want to, but realized he was the only one not transfixed by whatever it was they were looking at.

They were standing in the thin wedge of grass that separated the street from the park wall, in the shadows beneath trees that still flourished on this side, but were charred on the other. The streetlight above their heads had burned out a long time ago, and nobody had bothered to replace it.

Slowly, unwillingly, he looked up.

There was a boy sitting atop the wall. He had his back to them, his legs dangling over the opposite side. His hair was shorn to the bone, allowing them to see the network of pink scars on his scalp. He wore a threadbare brown and white striped T-shirt, and the way he rocked to and fro suggested he was swinging his legs contentedly.

"Hey, kid," Miguel said, but then Jelica grabbed his arm with her free hand, silencing him.

Don't, she advised.

As if the kid had mistakenly assumed her command was directed at him, he froze.

Conner felt the hair prickle on the back of his neck. *This is the start of it*, he thought. *This is it telling us it knows we're here.*

Yes, Jelica said. *And giving us a warning while there's still time to heed it.*

The kid, scalded by the shadows, turned his head to look down at them, and Conner felt horror flutter in his stomach like a trapped bird.

The child had no face, only a bloodless concavity within which nothing but darkness existed, like a shell from which the flesh of an egg has been removed.

"Oh God," Conner said.

"Call us whatever you wish," said the faceless child in a voice like rain drumming on a tin roof. He collapsed into a pile of ash the breeze was quick to carry away.

For a moment the three of them stood motionless, unable to speak. But then Jelica relinquished her vice-like grip on the two men's arms and headed deeper into the shadows and around the corner toward the main entrance on the east side.

It's just trying to scare us. The quaver in her voice was testament that it had succeeded in its task.

"Mission accomplished," Conner said and cast a glance at Miguel, whose expression indicated that they were in complete agreement. Nevertheless, they followed her lead, because even if they'd conceded to the overwhelming instinct to flee and never look back, there was no way either of them were going to leave Jelica to enter the 'Pines alone.

At the main gate, she stopped and waited for them.

"Are you really sure this is the best idea?" Conner asked when they reached her. "I mean, not that I'm doubting your abilities, but as far as I know, you've never been able to conjure faceless children out of ash. And if you're right, that little party trick was only a *warning*. What's it going to do when we get close to it and start our hoodoo, whip up a T-Rex?"

"Yeah," Miguel said. "Maybe we should come back with more people. People like the police, or the National Guard."

And how do you think that conversation starts? Jelica asked as she jangled the thick padlocked chain which hung from the handles on the tall sheet metal gates. *Sir, we desperately need your assistance in killing a particularly ill-behaved piece of the ground.*

Despite the fear, or perhaps because of it, Conner couldn't help himself. He sniggered into his fist, avoiding Miguel's scowl.

And besides, remember that it thrives on large numbers. The more people there are, the more it feeds. Try to remember what it was like growing up here, how slowly and insidiously it worked. Whatever it was doing, it drew it out over the years. It has no schedule, doesn't rush. It likes to take its time. And the more people there are, the more fun it is.

"This ground is a bit of a dick," Conner said, and now, amazingly, all three of them grinned. *Here we are, literally at the gates of Hell,* Conner thought, *and we're smiling.*

Once the brief but welcome moment of mirth abated, Miguel joined Jelica in inspecting the padlock. "I have a bolt cutter in my trunk that can take care of this if we need to."

Jelica shook her head. *If at possible, I'd prefer to avoid leaving any evidence that we were here.*

The odd way she spoke aroused Conner's suspicions. "Why's that?"

She shrugged nonchalantly. *Respect.*

Something greasy moved in Conner's gut. As far as he knew, she had never lied to him in all their years together, but he was certain that she was lying now. Worse, he thought he knew why. *She doesn't expect to make it out of here alive, and doesn't want us to be blamed for her death if someone discovers we were here.*

He opened his mouth to say something, maybe to demand they call this whole insane idea off while they still had the chance, but Jelica interrupted him by moving to the wall next to the gate.

Conner, give Miguel a boost up. He can hoist you up, then you can pull me up. Once we're over, we're in its domain, so be ready for anything.

"Jelica—"

She glared at him, and the anger in her eyes hurt.

I'm determined, Conner, as I'm sure you can tell. What you might not be able to tell is that I'm scared to death, just like you, and just like Miguel. But this has to be done, and the longer we stand around out here debating it, the more time we're allowing for doubt and second-guessing. Now let's move.

So he did, and a few moments later, they were sitting atop the wall much as the kid had done, though there was nothing innocent or casual in their postures, deceptive or otherwise. Nobody who bore witness to the blackened chaos spread out before them could possibly feel anything but sorrow, and now that he was seeing it with his own eyes for the first time, Conner felt a change in his emotions. Gone was the uncertainty, the fear tampered down into a cold spot in his chest. Sunny Pines had not been kind to him, and nobody had ever prospered here, but Jelica was right, it shouldn't have ended this way, and they should have done something to prevent it.

Sunny Pines

He didn't intend to make that same mistake again.

Whatever had poisoned the earth here needed to be dealt with once and for all.

"Let's get this done," he said through clenched teeth, and slipped off the wall into the inky darkness of the trailer park.

The others followed.

Four

Spent ash stained every surface inside the cinderblock walls surrounding Sunny Pines. Their feet stirred sooty plumes with every step.

Jelica shivered and Conner considered putting his arm around her but hesitated. She glanced at him from the corner of her eye, picking up his unguarded thoughts. Something passed between them in that brief glance, a charged energy that existed only when they were close to one another. He'd forgotten that feeling—a sensation akin to love, but somehow deeper, somehow more fragile—just as he'd forgotten to barricade his thoughts to keep her at a distance in the first place.

Jelica shoved her hands into her coat pockets and stepped ahead of Conner and Miguel, her hair a mass of red curls bobbing atop her backpack.

Miguel shrugged and followed her, then a couple of seconds later so did Conner. He took in the trailer park's familiar layout. The single track of cracked blacktop snaking through the ranks of trailers. The postage stamp playground that had never been clear of cigarette butts or layers of obscene graffiti. The short squat building that once housed the rental office and laundromat. The ominous phonebooth under the nearby light post.

Sunny Pines

Conner could almost see the man everyone called Uncle inside the booth, the phone to his ear as he lorded over the fiends lurking within the walls of Sunny Pines. Uncle with his chipped front tooth. Uncle with a smile that never left his eyes, even, rumor had it, when he sliced off Eddie Doherty's pinky finger for trying to sell an eighth of skunk weed he'd stolen from a rich high schooler. No one knew the truth behind that rumor, at least no one but Uncle and Eddie Doherty, but Eddie had disappeared a week after losing his finger, and Uncle himself saw no advantage to setting the record straight.

It was hard to deny the familiarity, the flood of muscle memory Conner felt as soon as he entered Sunny Pines, but this wasn't the run-down, desperate patchwork of trailers he'd left behind all those years ago. Fire had transformed the place he'd spent his youth into a wasteland of melted globs of metal and plastics, fabrics burned to delicate husks by torrents of flame, shattered glass blackened with ash scattered like buckshot.

It's so quiet, Conner thought, wanting to break the silence more than communicate directly with Jelica.

She turned to him and nodded. *I know. It's unsettling.*

"What's unsettling?" Miguel looked to Conner to fill in the gaps in their strange collective conversation.

"The silence," Conner replied.

It's... palpable, Jelica added. *Like the silence itself is breathing.*

"Yeah, true that," Miguel whispered. "Hey, remember that 4th of July?" he said with a nervous chuckle. "We sat on top of the wall and watched the fireworks from all the neighboring towns."

"Yeah, we shared a two liter of root beer and a package of red vines."

The sky was so clear, Jelica said, her voice whimsical within his head.

"Right?" Miguel said. "We watched eight or ten different fireworks displays, one after another."

Good times, Jelica said.

"The best," Conner added.

"You know, it's strange… " Miguel tilted his head back, his mouth slowly opening as they waited for him to continue. "When I drove out to meet you guys at the 7-Eleven, I remember thinking we were lucky. A clear sky, full of stars? At least we'd have the weather on our side tonight, you know? How'd I get it so wrong?"

Conner followed his friend's gaze to a sky as dark as pitch. He saw no hint of starlight, nor any clouds above them. Just darkness and some suggestion of serpentine movement.

This is bad, Jelica said.

"What do you mean? What's happening?" Conner said.

Movement within the darkness became evident, shadows roiling within waves of even darker night. It blanketed the sky from one cinderblock wall to the next.

This is how it all ends, she said, her voice trembling. *It's been waiting for us.*

No more than fifty feet away, the darkness funneled down from the sky. The charred earth crackled at its touch, sending ash rushing in every direction.

I'm so sorry, guys, Jelica said. *I should've left you out of this.*

"Don't say that. We're in this together," Miguel said, his shaky voice belying his words. "No matter what."

Conner felt paralyzed to say anything, to do anything more than to take hold of Jelica's hand. The leading edge of blown ash buffeted their faces. Smelling of sulfur and spoiled meat, it stung like the coldest winter's night.

We better get out of here, Jelica said, her face twisting at the stench.

Conner looked from the rolling waves of wintery ash heading straight for them, to Jelica's panic-stricken face. She tugged on his hand, but he didn't seem to have any control over his legs.

"Snap out of it, Bro." Miguel slugged Conner's shoulder.

Run! Jelica screamed so loud inside their heads that something popped inside Conner's ears. *Come on!*

She yanked on his hand once again and this time he moved. Frigid ash bit at their heels as they ran in the direction they had come, their backpacks jouncing on their shoulders. Another pillar of darkness funneled down directly in their path. They tried to route around it, but it was no use; the whole sky had become a sieve letting in columns of ash that rained down all around them.

The darkness was so absolute that Conner could no longer see the once familiar cinderblock walls. Just vague outlines of the pathway, the lone phonebooth, the management office in the near distance.

Miguel, gasping as he ran, said, "The... laundromat!"

What's the point? Conner thought.

We have to do something. We need time to think.

"We can do this," Miguel said, ever the positive one of the trio. "The three of us. Come on!"

The air crackled as the unremitting darkness spread. Miguel sprinted ahead, dodging one column and another, cutting angles like an all-pro running back. Conner and Jelica closed in, reaching the ruins of the laundromat a few seconds after Miguel.

"Hurry! Come on, come on!" Miguel urged, pinwheeling one arm while holding the door open with the other. His eyes widened as Jelica entered the laundromat, then he gave off a mournful choke when Conner passed him at the threshold. Conner immediately spun back toward the door to where Miguel stared in rapt horror at the sky.

Faces appeared in the darkness, emerging for a few seconds before ceding back into the growing horde as others took center stage. Faces full of torment, full of pain and despair. Sunny Pine faces.

Oh my God... Jelica said. *Miggy. No!*

"Jesus..." Conner understood immediately. Of the many faces to materialize and fall back into the murk, one lingered. One familiar to all three of them.

Bonita Ramos. Miguel's mother.

"Momma...?" Miggy's face pulled into an ugly fist of pain.

She stood as if floating on a rolling bed of black smoke, her normally bronze skin sickly gray and littered with seeping wounds. Soil

34

clung to her hair, and her fingernails were jagged and filthy, as if she'd just clawed free from the earth. She wore nothing but an oversized man's undershirt and it did little to cover the red scorpion tattoo on her upper thigh.

Miggy, don't look. Please, Miggy… it's not real, Jelica's voice trembled with uncertainty.

Bonita's shirt had been sliced in several places, mirroring the killing lashes she'd suffered at the hands of some unknown assailant when the three friends were still in high school. After the bus dropped him off one day, Miggy discovered her body in the alley behind their trailer, bludgeoned and sliced until she'd bled out.

"Miguelitto, my you've grown." She flashed a smile. While Bonita had always had a sweet yet tired smile, when her lips now parted that sweetness was gone. Her lone emotion was a barely controlled rage thrumming just beneath the surface. "So handsome you are."

"What's… what's happening?" Miguel said, his voice cracking. He glanced at Jelica, but quickly returned his gaze to the awful sight.

Don't listen to her, Miggy, Jelica said. *Whoever that is… whatever that is… it's not real.*

"Let me get a closer look at you…" Bonita pressed a cadaverous palm against the glass separating them. Even as tears welled in his eyes and his lips began to tremble, Miguel reached out for his dead mother.

"Don't do it, Bro." Conner wrapped his arms around him, holding him in a tight grip from behind. He turned to Jelica for help, but she backed away into the narrow gap between two burnt out washers, slumping down until she sat amongst the charred debris.

"Jelica!" Conner called out, but her eyes became glazed, distant and disbelieving.

"Oh, Jesus… Momma. Why are you doing this to me?"

"I missed you so much," Bonita said. "So very much."

Conner strained to shove Miguel away from the door. His friend had always been stocky as a boy, and with the hard labor of his working years, he'd become deceptively strong. He might as well have been rooted to the spot.

"Please… Miggy…" Conner said, struggling to move him.

Miguel pressed his palm against the glass, mirroring the corrupted flesh on the other side. Satisfaction gleamed in her eyes and her lips formed a victorious grin.

"Now, baby… let me in. I need you, Miguelitto. Need your big bear hugs. Remember when times were tough and you'd hug me with all your strength? How I'd comb my fingers through your hair and whisper stories to you about when I was a little niña in Ojinaga? About how my papa would work the cotton fields during the day and sing and play his accordion with different norteña bands at night?"

Miguel panted, straining against Conner's shoving while trying to rationalize his mother's presence.

"I need that now, more than ever. And I can see it in your eyes—so do you."

"Let go of me!" Miguel elbowed Conner in the gut, nearly knocking the wind out of him, but Conner held firm.

"Remember your abuelo? Nothing made him happier than his music. Nothing made him prouder than seeing his firstborn grandson taking his first steps. Remember when you'd have a nightmare, how he'd sing you to sleep while rocking you in his arms?"

"*Momma…*" The single word held a plea, a lament, a long-buried longing now set free.

"Remember our plans?" Bonita's smile widened, revealing gray teeth and blackened gums.

"It's impossible. You can't know this. Any of it. No one knows. Nobody but me and… *and…*" His face again crumpled.

"Of course I know of our plans, Miguelitto! All we ever talked about was moving back to that sleepy little village, and leaving this hellhole, this tierra de la muerte behind. You know what, Miguelitto? We can still do that. We can still be a family, together, in Ojinaga. I just need you to let me in."

Miguel reached for the deadbolt, a tear coursing down his cheek. "He's really there, Momma? Mi abuelo?"

"Yes, but of course! And with you and me, your Paulina, your own little niñas..." Bonita choked back a sob, "we can all be together forever... para siempre, Miguelitto. Para siempre."

Jelica, we gotta do something. Conner focused on projecting the thought at her as if he were throwing a baseball. She remained sitting between the washing machines, but he did notice her flinch, perhaps even from receiving his thought. *Jelica, please! I need you. We both need you!*

"But Momma... I saw you dead. Your skin was cold." The tension eased in slow degrees from Miguel's limbs. He pulled his hand away from the glass and looked at his palm as if it had deceived him. "I saw flies land in your mouth, on your naked eyes. I heard their buzzing, even in my dreams. Still do. I saw your coffin lowered into the ground. I cried, oh God I cried over what happened to you, Momma. It hurt... hurt so damned bad..."

"Oh, Miguelitto—"

"But that pain?" He sniffed, gathering up his courage. "That pain is what happens when you say goodbye to someone you love." He wiped snot from his nose. "This isn't you, Momma. This isn't *you.*"

Conner again pressed into Miguel's bulk, and this time he managed to separate him from the torturous image of his mother. The big man turned and clutched him, buried his face into his shoulder and cried as the full force of his sadness came to the surface.

The Bonita-thing's expression darkened, revealing its true vile nature.

As Miguel sobbed, Conner met Jelica's eyes. *Please, Jelica. We need you. I don't know what to do.*

Jelica took a fortifying breath and stood, wiping tears from her face. She clutched her hands close to her chest as if in prayer. Her lips moved a split second before he heard her words in his head:

You are not of this world, Jelica said, stepping forward. *This is not your place! You seek the weak to weaken them still. You wreak havoc among the defenseless, but nothing roots you to this diseased land. You destroyed all those who have come, everyone you touch.*

"Not all, Angelica," the Bonita-thing said, shifting its glare to her. "Not by a long shot. Not when people like you keep returning like a dog after its own sick."

Jelica's eyes widened with rage as she approached the glass.

"We never thought you'd come back. You, the most troubled of all the damned residing at Sunny Pines. And we… all of us…" the Bonita-thing said and spread her arms, the others milling closer to the glass, "are so glad you came."

Fuck you, Jelica said, anger tightening her voice.

"Oh, the mouth on you. So vile for someone without a voice."

I know what you are. I know what you do.

"If that's the case, then that just shows what you *are*, and what you *do*." The Bonita-thing exhaled against the glass and drew a heart in the frost. "Tell me, did you tell your friends what happened to your family?"

The Bonita-thing slammed her hand into the glass, sending spider web cracks stretching across its surface.

Without thinking, Conner jumped between the glass door and Jelica. He didn't know why he did it; the act was natural, pure instinct. Jelica pushed forward as if trying to get at the doorway, as if she would attack the thing on the other side of the glass with nothing but her fists, teeth, and fingernails, but he managed to hold her back, just barely. With her so close, he heard a whimper escape her, a wounded sound emanating from somewhere deep in her chest.

"Remember, Jelica, you said so yourself. It's not real," he said. "No matter what it says. It's not real!"

"Here's a lesson to remember: Jelica Palmer, the little section-8 trailer tramp, killed her family. Her husband, her two adorable kids. That's right, there wasn't any tragic car accident. No sir! Not even close. And she not only killed them, she knew she would kill them and did it anyway."

Jelica opened her mouth as if to scream; while no audible sound came, the violence in her thoughts hammered into Conner and Miguel like a physical blow. Their bodies went limp and they toppled to their sides like fresh-cut logs. Conner's shoulder crashed into the floor and his vision sparked brighter when his head bounced against the concrete.

He couldn't move, but he tasted blood as it pooled in the hollow of his slack cheeks. His ears felt plugged as if submerged under meters of water while his eyelids slurred through a series of prolonged blinks.

His unsteady gaze shifted from the rolling darkness outside the glass door to the tumbled over body of his friend. Miguel's eyes remained open, unmoving, vacant.

On the other side of the cracked windowpane, where the black ash was now retreating, Bonita Ramos was no longer there, if she had ever been there in the first place.

Conner could see nothing of Jelica, but she was nearby; he sensed her closeness, the charged energy he felt whenever they were near to one another. He tried to speak, but vocalization eluded him. As his thoughts drifted away, he hoped she could still hear his thoughts.

Before he lost consciousness, he realized—acknowledging for the first time—that what he felt for her was true love. He had never considered it to be anything more than a childhood crush until now because he had never experienced it either before meeting her or since their parting all those years ago. And what a tragedy to realize at this moment, his entire life he'd loved but one person.

He blinked, closed his eyes once again, and this time kept them closed. It would be so easy to never open them again. To never have to see this fouled place, this charred abyss where tormented souls lingered to feed on the living.

Five

The inside of Conner's eyelids blazed a honeyed crimson as he dozed in a lawn chair while waiting on Miggy. He smiled as the sun baked his skin and pollen tickled his nose.

Ah... summertime.

It wasn't just a word, but an emotion, the perfect marriage of freedom and unlimited possibility. The next twelve weeks were going to be a riot.

Somewhere nearby a lawnmower thundered to life, belching obscenely for all the world to hear.

No, not the entire world. Conner chuckled and opened his eyes. *Just here, at the 'Pines. And that's only 'cause Miggy Ramos doesn't live anywhere else.*

He sat up in his lawn chair, the frayed nylon webbing threatening to tear from dry rot at any moment. As if on cue, Miguel barreled around the corner of his mother's trailer, sitting astride the cobbled-together source of that horrible noise. Miguel waved enthusiastically and cut a shaky line toward him.

"You're freakin' crazy, Bro!" Conner stood from the lawn chair, sweat causing his skin to peel away from the nylon. "I can't believe you did it!"

Miggy had worked some kind of mechanical magic. Besides the original rusted out lawnmower, he'd added scraps of 2x4s, old bike frames, garage door cables, and who knows what else, to create a monstrosity that not only allowed him to ride and steer the mower, but amazingly, to actually cut the grass.

It wasn't like Mrs. Ramos had much of a yard around her trailer— nobody at Sunny Pines had more than ten feet of patchy grass skirting their tiny homestead, but Miggy wasn't having any part of pushing that mower more than the bare minimum.

Conner wouldn't admit it aloud, but he was jealous of the peach fuzz above Miguel's lip as well as the hair that nearly reached his shoulders. Conner's mother would never allow him such freedoms, but Miggy's mom didn't care what her son did as long as he got good grades, came home at night, and turned a blind eye to the demons plaguing her adult life: convenient store booze, cheap meth, the propensity to fall in and out of love on a dime.

She didn't have to worry about good ol' Miggy. Besides his shaggy appearance, he was about as straight-edged as anyone, especially someone from the 'Pines.

Miggy had started his little project a week ago, and the grass around his trailer had grown tall and weedy. It was a gamble to take on such a task, especially if he failed and somehow the mower wasn't usable afterwards. If he didn't get the mower up and running again, Mr. Entrican, the property manager, would soon come around to harass his mom with offers to mow it in exchange for certain lurid services in return. It wasn't uncommon to see the stooped little man mowing trailer park grass from sunup to sundown as sweat streamed down his perpetually grinning face.

Miguel wasn't ignorant about how his mom paid her bills, but he wasn't about to add to her burden by taking their only working mower permanently out of commission. From the looks of things, Mr. Entrican would have to ply his skeevy trade elsewhere.

"Told ya, Bro!" Miggy took his hand off the makeshift steering wheel and pumped his arm. The mower started to twist and nearly toppled him before he took hold of the wheel and righted it again.

"You crazy pendejo!" Conner shouted to be heard over the rumbling motor spitting gray smoke into the air.

Miguel feigned hurt and turned off the mower by releasing a handle at the steering wheel. The entirety of Sunny Pines returned to its drowsy summertime quiet. "Hey, you can't call me that!"

"Don't you usually call me cracka'?"

"Point taken." They laughed and bumped fists. "Well, this pendejo isn't gonna get used to pushing a lawnmower for nobody, even his own mother." Miguel smiled and tugged on his shirt sleeve to mop his brow.

Conner nodded. "I can see that."

"You might want to mow your own grass before Mr. Entrican comes looking for your momma with that creepy grin on his ugly mug."

"I'll get to it when I get to it. Besides, Jerry's scary enough to keep Entrican from getting any ideas."

Miguel grunted. "Lucky you."

"Yeah, lucky me." Conner lifted his shirt, revealing a mass of healing bruises along his ribcage. "The dickhead felt bad about it, so the last week's been pretty easy, but that edge is coming back to his eye."

"Maybe you should just zip your lip and avoid eye contact."

"That's some way to live."

"Well, I'd take having to tap dance around a crazy stepdad over walking in on some pimple-assed businessmen giving it to my mom on his lunchbreak."

"Let's just call it a tie. We both got shitty lives." Conner picked a long blade of grass and stuck one end between his teeth. "How about you hurry the hell up," he said, chewing on the grass. "I want to head to town and sneak into the Apollo."

"What's playing?"

"Does it matter? It's better than hanging out here, right?"

"Fine, but this mofo has one speed." Miguel pulled the draw cord and the mower rumbled to life and clouded the air between them with its gray smoke.

"And with your fat ass, it'll only get slower."

Miguel grinned and flipped him the bird as he steered down the long stretch parallel to his mom's trailer.

Conner spat out the blade of grass as he went back to his lawn chair and sat down to wait for him to finish up. He considered dragging his own mower from his shed to get the mowing out of the way, but he figured the guilt over his latest beating would get Jerry to do it at least one more time.

He couldn't wait to get out of this place. The 'Pines was a dead end. No one ever seemed to leave except in a coffin. Everyone wanted to be somewhere else, but something always held them in check, keeping them moored to their trailers, tied to their networks of dealers, pimps, and broken family members.

The Apollo in the middle of town was one of the only escapes for Conner and Miguel. They justified their sneaking into the theater by reasoning that they never actually stole anything, at least not physically. They never snuck in when a show was going to sell out; that would've been stealing the ticket price from the theater owner. They figured they were merely keeping otherwise empty seats warm. And while they never stole from the concession stand, it wasn't beneath them to eat from a half empty bucket of popcorn left behind in one of the creaky old seats. While it wasn't stealing anything physical, the act of seeing the movies would often bring them enough joy or escapism to get through another week, another month of living in the 'Pines. Regardless—if it was or wasn't stealing—it didn't matter. They took advantage of it whenever they could get away from the trailer park.

When they were both nine they'd discovered the door at the top of the Apollo's fire escape didn't latch properly. They'd been looking for a secret spot to launch Miggy's homemade paper airplanes without getting bullied by bigger kids. While they'd both meticulously folded and refolded scraps of paper into a myriad of flying machines, Conner's never looked right, always looked somehow askew, while Miguel could build just about anything, and off the top of his head, and every detail of his creations would be crisp and accurate, and in its crispness and accuracy, it would be beautiful as well. So, while they both brought planes to the Apollo, in truth, they both wanted to witness Miggy's creations cut through the air.

The Apollo building was just about as tall as any in town, and the parking lot next door afforded a wide open airspace for the planes to fly through.

It was just a matter of cracking the door open, listening for people in the darkened corridor leading to the main theater, and a quick silent scamper to the entrance to the balcony seats. No matter how sticky the floors got, or how crackly the speakers became, the place was usually hopping every weekend and even most weekdays during summer. Their sudden appearance had never raised an eyebrow.

As far as Miguel and Conner knew, this secret was theirs and theirs alone. They treasured it and kept it to themselves. When they opened the door to the vast and empty darkness of the theater, it opened to a world of possibilities.

Miguel came around again on his mower, and when he did, he held up his index finger and mouthed: *One more loop.*

Conner gave him a thumbs up and sat back, ready to let his mind drift for another five minutes until Miguel wrapped things up.

Even with the rumble and groan of Miguel's homemade riding mower, Conner still heard the van's muffler as it pulled up the final curve in the cracked blacktop before it rolled to a sputtering stop in front of the trailer sandwiched between Conner's and Miguel's. No one had occupied the faded mint green doublewide since Jinny Boatright died from a heroin overdose sometime the previous Christmas. Mr. Entrican had found her cold and alone when he'd come by three days into the new year to either collect her three-month overdue rent, or start the eviction process.

The van coughed gouts of black exhaust and the engine pinged even after it was shut off. While Conner had felt nothing in Jinny's passing, he did feel stirrings of anger at seeing a new batch of neighbors ready to shrink his world with their presence. He'd enjoyed the added sense of seclusion since Jinny's passing, and no one bothered to yell at him for cutting across the twenty feet of weedy grass to see Miguel.

He was ready to pass judgment and hate these new neighbors when the van's side door opened wide and two girls climbed out. One girl was tall and had dark hair and pale skin. She wore short shorts, a sky blue tank top that bared her flat belly. She lugged a canvas duffle bag onto her shoulder and sneered directly at Conner when she noticed his stare.

Conner offered her a smile and she replied with a dramatic eye roll, a raised middle finger, and a sharp-edged cold shoulder as she turned toward the trailer.

The brunette bumped into the second girl, a slim redhead with dark freckles on her nose and cheeks.

Do you always have to be such a snot? a girl's voice said.

Conner jumped in his seat. He heard the words as if they'd been whispered in his ear. He found himself blushing as he turned around each direction, but there was no way someone could have snuck up on him.

The redhead glared at the brunette, who dropped her duffle and started chewing on a fingernail as she stood on the single step leading to the trailer door. He supposed he could've misheard her, at least the location of the sound of her voice—her expression did match the tone of what he'd heard—but he didn't see how it was possible.

It's not like any of us want to be here, the voice said. This time, as he stared at the pale pink of the redhead's lips, he was certain she hadn't spoken aloud. *You're nothing special. You're always such a spoiled brat.*

The driver's side door opened and flakes of rust sloughed off the van's frame. A tired woman of indeterminate age stepped out. She stretched her back in an arch and let out a long sigh that seemed to deflate her by a third by the time she'd finished. The years had been unkind to her. She could've been the girls' mother or grandmother, or perhaps one of each to each of the girls.

Conner didn't notice Miguel had shut down his mower, so it startled him when his friend came over and sat on the boulder next to Conner's front door.

"I'll take my ten dollars in small bills."

"Ten dollars? For mowing your own grass?" Conner scoffed without looking away from the new arrivals.

Noticing the girls, Miguel whispered his reply: "We made a bet, remember? You didn't think I'd make my own riding mower."

"Yeah, right. Forgot about that. How about I take you to a movie, we'll call it even?"

"Whatever, dude." Miguel slugged his shoulder.

The woman glared at the pair. "What're you lookin' at?"

"Nothing." Conner's cheeks burned crimson when the brunette looked over and shook her head at him. "Nothing at all."

"Let's keep it that way," the woman said as she went to the back door of the van. She groaned as she hefted a plastic laundry basket from inside. A baby squawked from inside it, pathetic and weak. A second voice joined the first. "And I mean both of you. Don't need no white trash or fat ass beaner sniffing around my daughters. I got two guns and a box cutter. I'll use 'em all, but you'd count yourself lucky if I'm only within reach of a gun."

"Yes…" Conner began before his voice cracked. The babies in the laundry basket cried louder.

"… Ma'am," Miguel added, nodding in agreement.

The redhead stood aside to let her mom pass so she could open the door.

"Marilyn, take this basket of belly-achin' so I can get the damn key out."

The brunette rolled her eyes, but she took possession of the laundry basket and her expression softened when she looked down. The babies cried in unison and she shushed them.

Miguel and Conner stared openly as the woman unlocked the door and bumped it open with her shoulder. "Jesus… Jelica, get in here and open a blasted window. Smells like death in here."

Conner shuddered, thinking of Jinny.

The redhead brushed her hair behind her ear before disappearing into the trailer.

"She's just…" Conner sighed, "amazing."

"The brunette?" Miguel said. "Yeah, she's definitely a hotty, but she knows it. I don't know if that makes her hotter or just the opposite."

"No, not her. The redhead. Jelica. That's what her mom said. *Jelica,*" he repeated, the name flowing like musical notes off his tongue.

Miguel cocked an eyebrow. "That skinny thing?"

The curtains flew open and Jelica lifted the window in its sash. Her brow was furrowed as she glared unwaveringly at Miguel.

"What's she doing?" Miguel said from the side of his mouth.

"She's staring at you, pendejo. I think she heard you."

Jelica put one hand on her narrow hip. *I'm not that skinny. At least I'm not—*

"Jesus!" Conner said, his mouth gaping wide.

"Did you hear that?"

"Her lips didn't even move."

Jelica jumped out of view.

"That just happened, didn't it?" Conner said.

"What are we, some kind of mind readers now?"

The door to the trailer opened, but no one immediately came out. The mother, agitated, barked orders at the two girls, barked at the two babies to shut the hell up, barked oaths to unseen gods, prayers to anybody listening.

"Marilyn, get up off your ass and help me—don't you give me that look!" the woman yelled. "I'll slap it right off your lilywhite face!"

Miguel turned to Conner, mouthed: *Oh my god!*

Conner replied: *I know!*

She's not that bad, the girl's voice spoke inside Conner's head as clear as day. Miguel slugged his shoulder as if to get his attention.

"Dude, enough with the punches!" Conner rubbed his shoulder.

"This is seriously bizarro world."

She's just… Jelica said, *she's just had a string of bad luck. If you can hear me, think your names.*

Conner again turned to Miguel, who could only shrug.

After a few seconds, she replied. *Conner and… Miguel? So you two can hear me?*

"Yes," Conner and Miguel said at the same time.

Can you hear each other's thoughts?

"No, thank God," Conner said, chuckling.

Miguel grunted. "Yeah, gross."

They waited, and after a few drawn out seconds of silence, Jelica stepped back out into the sunshine.

The sun danced on gold filaments trapped in the curls of her red hair. When Conner saw the brilliant blue of her eyes, his heart skipped a beat. His thoughts weren't coherent, but his feelings were a torrent of hormones that he had little control over.

Jelica's cheeks flushed and she had to look away from him. She smiled with her downturned gaze, and took a deep breath before looking at them both.

I'm Jelica. I've been waiting so long to find others, you know, people who can hear me. I've never been able to communicate this way with anyone besides my Great Aunt Pia. She died when I was little, so it's nice having someone else hear my voice.

"Jelica?" Conner turned to Miguel, wishing for once that he could send his thoughts to his friend.

Yes?

"Do you want to go to the movies with us?"

That'd be great… Her smile faded. *But I'm broke.*

"Don't worry about that." Miguel smiled. "It'll be our treat."

Miguel and Conner bumped fists.

That night they brought Jelica to the Apollo. They snuck in like they always had. When they entered the darkened hallway at the top of the fire escape, Jelica took hold of Conner's hand, and from that moment on, he could always feel her at his side.

Six

Conner? Jelica said and shook him. He felt her hand on his cheek and he pressed into its softness. *Can you hear me?*

He tried to move his limbs. While they did move, he seemed hardly in control of their movement. He couldn't even open his eyes.

Oh, God, I missed you so much. Why did I ever let you leave me?

He couldn't tell if it was his own internal voice, or Jelica's. Perhaps it was even both at once. This thought made him smile, both inside and out. He felt her finger trace his upturned lips as he drifted off again.

Seven

The light posts along the road outside Sunny Pines bled halos of tepid light inside the cinderblock walls—the hint of something better forever out of reach.

Kids had vandalized the streetlights within the trailer park so often that Mr. Entrican no longer bothered to replace them. No point in providing light to those who prefer traipsing the darkness. The 'Pines lone undamaged streetlight was the one high above Uncle's phonebooth, and no one dared to take away his spotlight.

Most of the residents stayed inside at night, but with their home lives in constant disarray, Conner and Jelica would often walk among the trailers long after nightfall. Tonight, just after midnight, they'd snuck out and now walked shoulder to shoulder, veering well clear of Uncle's spotlight until they reached the playground. Without exchanging a thought, Jelica sat on the nearest swing. Conner gave her a gentle push, glad the near dark hid the vulgar graffiti scribbled on every surface of the playground equipment.

They'd gotten close in the last couple of years—not in a dating sense—but still close enough they didn't always need words or thoughts to know what the other was thinking. Even though they weren't dating, they never invited Miggy on any of their late night walks, nor did the subject ever come up when the three were together. And while Conner had asked Jelica out more than once, she always turned him down by saying she didn't want to be with anyone until she was old and gray. After her latest rejection, he decided he'd wait patiently for her to come around. Well, as patient as any sixteen-year-old boy could be.

A dog barked nearby, yelped as if struck, then went quiet.

"It's getting cold," he said after a prolonged easy silence. "Shouldn't we get going?"

Never. Let's stay here forever, she said. Her curls fell over one eye as she turned to look at him. She grinned and the gleam in her eye warmed his heart, but something beneath the surface put him on edge.

"What's wrong?"

Besides everything? Her grin abruptly vanished.

He went around to face her, and when she approached him on the upswing, he took hold of her feet, suspending her in mid-air. She wouldn't look at him.

"Jelica…" he said, then continued in thought… *you know you can tell me anything. I mean it. I won't judge.*

She looked up, staring at his blackened right eye. Jerry had thrashed him good yesterday, so the swelling was still fresh. She didn't ask him about it. She avoided outwardly asking him about his constant bruises, scrapes, or odd injuries. But he knew she knew. It was hard to hide the truth from a girl who can hear your thoughts.

She pursed her lips and nodded. *Okay…*

He let go of her feet and gave the bottom of her shoes a gentle nudge. The chains squeaked softly as she moved.

Do you remember when I told you my mom gave the twins up for adoption?

He walked back behind her and pressed his hands into her lower back, enjoyed her closeness for a brief moment, and then let her fly away. "Yeah. That sucked."

Well… I lied. I'm sorry, but I barely knew you back then. I didn't want to admit how fucked up my family is.

"Jelica, wait a sec—"

Don't interrupt or I won't be able to get this all out. And I think... I really think I need to get it out, you know? Either that or take it with me.

"What's that supposed to mean?"

She didn't answer him, but he didn't need to hear her voice inside his head to understand. She meant what she meant; she would take whatever was eating at her away. In the parlance of the 'Pines that usually meant taking a hot bath with a cold razor.

I couldn't tell anyone, could never admit that I knew what really happened. Yeah, my mom could never take care of them... any of us, really. We weren't always just a couple of meals away from hunger. Sometimes we were just plain hungry. Sometimes there wasn't anything in our cabinets, and sometimes there wasn't electricity to keep the fridge going.

She paused and looked away in shame, as if she bore all the responsibility for what her mother could or could not provide. He kneeled in front of her, wrapping her hands in his. She was ice cold, colder than the midsummer air warranted. He said nothing.

So, yeah, we were hungry. And my mom didn't know where else to turn, not without having to confront her own demons. And who wants to do that, right? She chuckled, though tears filled her eyes.

He squeezed her hands, urging her on.

Mom... she asked Uncle for help. I heard her clear as day. Why do people at Sunny Pines act like their walls are soundproof? I hear everything happening three trailers away. Everybody's in everybody else's business. Like, all the time. So, yeah, I heard Mom talking to Uncle out back behind our trailer. And the very next day those squabbling little baby monsters were gone. Just... gone. Like they never existed.

"No way!"

She nodded and inhaled deeply, her chest hitching with emotion as she slowly let it out.

And you know what else happened? Not only was our fridge cold that very day, but there was milk and cheese inside. And the cabinets were full from the Pick 'N Save. And Mom, she was happy. So very happy. Either to be rid of the burden, or the quality of her score. She'd never been happier, high or not. At least not that I can remember.

A tear fell down her cheek and he brushed it gently away with the back of his hand.

She finally looked him in the eye. *So, what I'm trying to say is... I'm leaving.*

"What? You can't leave." Conner's heart hurt. He felt winded, angry even, but panicked most of all.

But I have to. I can't let this place ruin me.

"It won't if you don't let it." His voice sounded pathetic to his own ears, but he couldn't help it. "What... what are you going to do?" He wanted to shield the next thought: *What am I going to do without you?* but he couldn't stifle it before it slipped through and she heard it as clear as his spoken voice.

I don't know. Live? She tried to smile, but it looked more like a wince. *Does it matter?*

Conner stepped away from the swings, needing distance, needing space just to breathe. The chain squeaked as she stood. She approached and he thought she would place a hand on his shoulder. She didn't.

Remember when Marilyn ran away not long after we moved in? Things were better for a little while. Mom seemed to have her head on straight. She got that late-night job waitressing at the Hobo Lounge. Sure, I had to keep an eye on my brothers after she tucked them in at night, but money was steady for once. It was like the whole Marilyn thing was a wakeup call for Mom.

He turned to face her. Sure, he could hear her thoughts, but he lost the nuance without seeing her face.

That's enough to make you really think, to make you consider your life, your family.

"Sure, but she didn't stay clean. She fell off the wagon——"

Boy, did she ever... Almost died even.

"And then, it was just you and your brothers, and we now both know how that turned out."

The thing is... She sniffed back a tear. *I'm starting to think Marilyn didn't run away.*

56

Ray Garton   Bev Vincent   Kealan Patrick Burke   **Glen Krisch**

"Seriously?" Conner halfway understood what she was getting at, but he didn't want to believe a parent could be so cruel to disregard and discard her children one by one.

After what happened to my brothers? How could I not think she somehow sold off Marilyn to the highest bidder, or at least a bidder willing to trade some quality H for a young piece of ass?

"Jelica, I'm sure that's not what happened. I'm sure—"

Really... how can you know?

"Well, I guess... I don't know." He drew her close. He thought: *I'm sorry. Sorry for everything.*

So that's why I have to leave. If I stay, I'll wind up chained in some pervert's basement. Or I'll kill her. Whatever happens, it's not a pretty ending for me.

"I'll come with you."

You can't do this to me. Please... don't do this to me.

"Then, you stay. I'll kill her. I'll kill him, too. Someone needs to put an end to all this. I'll set things right."

She sighed. *Uncle isn't the monster. My mother isn't the monster. The monster... I think it's in all of us. Every single one of us. Not just here in the 'Pines. Everywhere. It's just something about this place. This land... it's like it's a doorway where only evil passes.*

"Yeah. I think you're right." He hugged her hard, not wanting to let go. "And something about this place. It feeds that evil. Gives it life, a warm place to rest its head." If he had to never see her again to allow her to escape the 'Pines, he would. No matter how much her absence would leave a void behind. "I can't imagine living here without you."

You'll get away. Somehow, you'll get away.

"Promise?" he whispered.

She nodded, sniffed again.

The warm scent of her hair weakened his knees. What would he do without her? No matter how hard he tried to block the thought, it escaped into the ether: *Please, don't leave me.*

57

Sunny Pines

Jelica flinched in his arms, but she said nothing in reply. Something had changed between them. Something had broken. Sharing one's company wasn't enough to overcome the sudden awkwardness.

They parted ways, each slinking back to their respective trailers. Conner wouldn't see Jelica for over twenty years.

Eight

Conner's eyes fluttered before opening to near darkness. Jagged pain shot through his skull, and the acrid stench of burning filled his nostrils. He grimaced but he couldn't escape it. Nothing at Sunny Pines had been left unscathed.

Shh… Jelica's gentle fingers traced his stubbled cheek, dulling the edges of the pain. *Thank God,* she said. *I was so worried.*

"Me too." His eyes had barely adjusted to the darkness; all he saw was the beautiful oval of Jelica's pale, freckled face above his, her auburn curls the extent of his vision.

"How is…" Conner croaked and moved to sit up. He immediately regretted it as pain shot from the base of his skull to his eyeballs.

Take it slow.

He eased back on his elbows. "Miggy. How's Miggy?"

"Like I got the worst hangover of my life," Miguel called out from the darkness. "Worse than that time we killed a fifth of Everclear when we were seventeen. But, you know, I'm alive, so I guess I got that going for me."

"You had to bring up the Everclear, didn't you?" It sounded so good to hear his old friend. Despite the circumstances, Conner couldn't help laughing. At the peak of it, his head throbbed and his vision started to pulse in time with his heartbeat.

You two... Jelica said with motherly exasperation. She smiled and pushed her hair behind her ear. She drifted from his sight, and Miguel's face filled his vision.

"We're unbelievable, right? Like two peas in a pod?" Conner slowly sat up, and as he moved, Miguel hooked an arm around his back until he was sure he wouldn't fall over.

"You okay?"

"Yeah, Bro."

The surroundings hadn't changed at all despite whatever trauma had knocked Conner flat out unconscious. The laundromat's six washers and dryers, three to a row—all charred and dead. The cinderblocks bearing not only the scars from the recent fire, but also the odd stray bullet hole, the splotches of white paint intended to cover lude graffiti somehow surviving the fire. The community announcement board, which had always reflected the health and well-being of the community, or lack thereof, continued to act out that role. Its singed cork backing blackened to cinders, the posted messages now just wisps of ash clinging to melted push-pins.

"So she's... your, um... Bonita's gone?"

"I sure the hell hope so," Miguel said.

I don't know what came over me, Jelica said with some embarrassment and confusion. *What happened. What I did.*

"Whatever it is you did, it worked," Conner said. "Look..." He pointed to the front windows, the glass door spider-webbed with cracks.

"She's really gone," Miguel said with relief.

It wasn't a she. That wasn't your mom.

"I know." Miguel stood, a bit unsteadily, before turning to Conner and offering him a hand up as well. They both grunted and sighed like men much older than they were. "But if that ever happens to you, just try to deny it, the emotions, *everything.* She knew things... stuff that only I knew, that my mom knew. It'll fuck with your head."

Ray Garton   Bev Vincent   Kealan Patrick Burke   **Glen Krisch**

The evil of this place will use anything to get to us. It's what brought us all back together in the first place.

"What is it?" Conner let his gaze wander, let the question linger. After a prolonged silence, when he started to strain his internal hearing for Jelica's voice, he turned to face her, but she turned away, as if ashamed. "What does it want?"

I'm not entirely sure. But it needs to feed. Its appetites have gotten… out of control, I guess you could say.

"But why us? Why this land, this… what did the natives call it?"

"A black spot," Miguel said.

"Right. Why couldn't the shamans rid this land of the black spot?"

I've learned over the years, evil can be defeated, but only if it is finite.

Conner checked the deadbolt, the one which Miguel nearly opened to let in whatever evil had taken on the appearance of his dead mother. Luckily, it was closed. "And whatever this evil is, it's not finite?"

Miguel shook his head. "I can't even wrap my mind around this. Any of it. It's bonkers. Like, I can't ever mention any of this to Paulina. She'd check me in to the loony bin herself."

Let's say you walk into your kitchen to get a midnight snack. Jelica paused and raised one knowing eyebrow at Miguel. *No one knows what you're up to. Especially the mouse that's eating the crackers in the cupboard.*

"You saw that, didn't you?" Miguel said, his mouth gaping. "That happened to me a couple nights back. And when you pulled up at the 7-Eleven I was thinking about that little shit looking all innocent on the cupboard shelf holding a saltine in its tiny paws."

It's the first thought I heard from you. In all those years, that's the thought you send out my way? What the hell, man? Where's the creativity?

"I was just freaked out about its beady little eyes and couldn't shake the thought."

I know. And you killed the little shit. You swatted at him with your hand and when he went scampering across the kitchen tile, you reached down for your work boot and let it fly. Jelica shivered as if she had just witnessed the result herself.

"Lucky shot."

Conner elbowed Miguel. "Not for the little shit mouse."

No. And I hate to break it to you, Miggy, but there's probably dozens of those little shits in the walls of your house. In the ceiling.

"Jesus, don't make me puke."

It might not be the case. But it most likely is. Mice aren't solitary creatures.

Miguel shook his head. "And we're talking about the rodent infestation at my house because?"

Mice aren't solitary creatures, and neither are the evil spirits feeding off the living here at the 'Pines. I don't think they're from this world, this universe even. I think they travel through a portal, or black spot as the shamans would call it, in order to feed, and the only way they reach our world is to ride the spirit of the lingering dead. They take possession of the spirit—

"What, like a parasite?" Conner cut in.

Yeah, that makes sense. And when they do, they turn the spirit sour. It amplifies the negativity inherent to that person's life.

"And these evil... little shits, they're in the walls, the ceilings, so to speak?"

"Yeah, and when the lights go out, they roam free, seeking sustenance."

Miguel shuddered. "Momma... they have her. She's trapped. And this whole time she hasn't been able to stop it. And it just feeds, and feeds, and her soul suffers, is drained of any... I guess my Paulina would call it... *grace.*"

And that's why we're here. Why we need to defeat them, to close the fucking black spot to wherever-the-hell forever.

"If we defeat whatever this evil is, however the hell we pull that one off, it'll be because of whatever's in these backpacks?" Miguel held up his pack by the strap.

Conner unzipped his own backpack and looked inside. "Is this some kind of joke? I'm supposed to battle whatever the hell those... those things are... with chalk?" He raked his fingers through his hair, dumbfounded.

From his own pack Miguel pulled out an odd assortment of hand tools—metal-cutting shears, a small pocket torch, a set of crescent wrenches—and set them on top of a charred washing machine. He raised a quizzical eyebrow.

See, it's not what's in the bag that will help us defeat this evil once and for all. Not really, at any rate. It's us. The three of us. It has something to do with when we're close together. You know, like the special way we communicate? Has that ever happened to either of you with anyone else?

Conner turned to Miguel. They both shook their heads.

It's like the three of us together multiplies our individual capabilities. Jelica picked up the torch. *This thing here? I have no idea what to do with it. With anything that's in that pack.*

"Then how did you decide what to bring?"

I trusted my gut. It told me, Miggy will know what to do with it, and when.

Miguel let out a defeated groan. "I have no idea what I'm supposed to do."

Yes, you do. It's inside you. You will work your mechanical genius.

"And, what am I supposed to do with chalk?" Conner emptied the pack. He hadn't used chalk in his work since art school, but this wasn't the high-quality chalk he would've used back then. All told, there were four plastic cartons of a dozen thick sidewalk chalks. This was kids' stuff.

When did you start drawing? When did the artistic bug bite?

"I don't know." He'd always considered himself a late bloomer in that regard. Most artists are born with it in their blood. Sure, they improved over time, through exertion, practice and repetition, but Conner could've given a rip about art until sometime in his late teens.

"It was right after my mom died," Miguel said. "You sketched that rose, remember? And you wrote at the bottom—"

May you find peace, Jelica cut in.

"Right… How could I have forgotten? That was really what started it all. I'd never really even tried to sketch anything. Like, anything at all.

63

And then, with the passing of your mom, I don't know… it's like something inside me needed to speak, to get out…"

And that's why I packed your pack that way. Your artistic ability is equal to Miggy's genius with machinery and mechanics.

"And you figured this out how?" Miguel said, his voice straining at the incredulity of their situation. "Did some expert on haunted land and interdimensional quote, unquote *little shit mice* impart his shamanistic wisdom on you?"

No, not exactly. She turned toward the front window and placed her palm against the cracked glass as if checking for a heartbeat.

"Why are we here, Jelica?" Conner asked.

This place, its evil has been calling me. She caressed the glass as she might a lover. She faced them, her eyes steely, the pale blue turned to ash and char. *Somehow, it infected my husband.*

It started when my mom came for a visit. I fought long and hard with Gary, but I finally caved to his thinking. How could I be so cruel to deny a grandmother the chance to see her grandkids? A few months earlier I'd received a handwritten letter with no return address, and while the handwriting was shakier than I remembered, it was unmistakable. Mom had found me. My family.

Conner had the urge to embrace her, to try to ease the suffering evident in the lines on her face, the fatigue in her eyes. Jelica glared at him and shook her head. Conner folded his arms and waited for her to continue.

I never responded to her letter. Gary didn't even know that she was alive, let alone that she'd reached out to me. But he came across the letter a month or so after it arrived. He questioned me about why I hid the letter, and then I tried to deny that something was wrong. But he knew.

Conner nodded. "I could always tell when you'd had a fight with her."

"Rattled," Miguel added. "You'd look rattled, to the core."

I guess I never lost that reaction. It'd just been dormant all those years. And in truth, after I moved away I'd go months, years even, without thinking about her or this place. I didn't know if she was alive or dead all those years, and it didn't matter, because she no longer existed in my world.

"But then, she found you."

I think it must've been from an article written about the vineyard. I of course took my husband's name, not wanting that final tie to my past. But, I don't know... she trailed off.

"Jelica."

Yes?

"Your name. It's unique. That's how she found you."

Yeah, I guess. I don't know why I didn't just change it along with everything else.

"So... did you invite her to visit?" Miguel asked.

No. God, no. I felt like a terrible person about denying her, as well as for arguing with Gary about it, but I couldn't bring myself to even respond to her letter. She took that choice out of my hands by showing up on our front steps—

The sudden sound of thunder rumbled outside, cutting her off mid-sentence. They all looked at one another, uncertain what was happening. The sound multiplied, but it wasn't just outside anymore. It was so prevalent, so violent, that the walls of the laundromat trembled, stirring up ash and sending up a storm of masonry dust and debris.

The ceiling began to cave in all around them. "Jelica!" Conner called out and reached for her.

Jelica held her arms above her head, looking for clear passage in the ten feet separating them.

The windows shattered inward, showering them with shards of glass. In one great span, the remains of the roof stagger-step collapsed by a foot, then by another foot and a half. From the remains of the windows, black smoke billowed inside the building, filling the gaps between falling debris, snaking through every crack and divide, every ounce of unsullied air.

"Jelica!" Conner choked on the dust. A ceiling tile and its aluminum framing crashed into him, staggering him. He was lucky that his backpack took the brunt of the impact.

Miguel grabbed his arm. "Let's get out of here!"

"Where is she! Where's Jelica?"

"I don't know, Bro. We'll find her, but right now we gotta go!"

Sunny Pines

Ropy tendrils of smoke lashed around Conner's arms, then his ankles. Tightening, they yanked him off his feet, dragging him through the collapsing remains of the laundromat. By chance, he caught sight of Miguel, who was being similarly manhandled. Conner strained with all his might to wrench free from the darkness, but its strength was absolute and unyielding. And as it dragged him bodily toward the shattered windows, the cinderblocks of the front wall caved inward, falling on him like a toppled domino.

Nine

Conner blinked and scurried to a sitting position. As he tried to orient himself, tiny flecks of ash began to settle as the weak light of dawn hesitantly breeched the walls of Sunny Pines. The laundromat had fallen in on him, knocking him flat against a bank of clothes washers. An amalgam of ceiling tiles, cinderblocks, and chunks of tarpapered roofing materials created a malformed dome above him. While he considered himself lucky to be alive, he didn't come away from the collapsed roof unscathed.

His right shoulder sloped inches below his left, and the slightest movement jolted the ruined socket with the pain of a red-hot poker. Shafts of dusty sunlight streamed into the tiny alcove. He tried to lift his arm but the resulting pain blurred his vision for a few seconds.

"Help!" he called out, and immediately coughed from the dust and ash. "Miggy…? Jelica?"

He coughed again, spat a gob of blackened phlegm.

Conner? Are you okay?

He'd never felt more relieved hearing another voice.

"Jelica," he said, then thought: *I'm trapped. I don't know what happened.*

She started crying, and the sound was worse than silence.

Sunny Pines

I didn't kill my family, she said. *Yes, I put a bullet in the head of whoever shared my bed at night, whoever slept in my kids' beds. But they were no longer my family. They hadn't been in a long time. Not since that visit with my mother. I hope you believe me and know there was nothing to be done about it. She took them from me. What I had to do... what I had to do was a mercy.*

Conner pressed against the rubble surrounding him, but it was an unmovable mass, as if it had been constructed that way. Dust scorched his throat as he strained. He eased off and looked for a different way out. There was none. He was trapped.

I should've never let her into my home. But I did. And she stayed for a perfectly pleasant week. There was not one instance of conflict. No dredging up the past. No hint of her being high or needing to be. She was just... a normal mother. We made salads together, for goodness sake. We walked the vineyard at night. We talked about the future... always the future.

Conner scraped his fingertips across the ground, scoring claw marks in the dust. He scraped and dug and persisted, whittling away at what trapped him.

And as we parted ways, just as soon as I closed the door and the taxi whisked her away to the airport, my family changed. That very moment they became not *my family, but something else, something tainted and rotting.*

Instead of picking me bouquets of flowers and presenting me with interesting little twigs or brightly-colored bird feathers, my kids brought me the mangled remains of squirrels and rabbits, their hands still warm and tacky with blood.

Instead of caressing me with affection, Gary beat me for the first time in our relationship. He then... he then degraded me. He—

Jelica... please don't, he broke in. *I don't need to know. I just need... I just need to know you're okay.*

I'm not okay. I've never been okay.

What are we going to do, Jelica? What can we do?

He first heard, then felt the building materials trapping him begin to stir. They awakened, moved as if compelled to do so.

"Jelica?"

The shafts of sunlight shifted, expanding and brightening as a path to freedom revealed itself. He couldn't do anything more than stare, mesmerized, as the plaster, drywall, veins of electrical conduits, cinderblocks, ceiling tiles—everything—between where he lay and the pitch-black sky above moved, was forced aside by some unseen force.

Before his way out collapsed again, he cradled his injured arm against his chest and crawled through the wreckage, through the desecration of what should have been sacrosanct—the land of his childhood.

He stood and gasped to catch his breath.

Jelica, he thought. "Jelica… where are you?"

He heard a rasping cough and he took off in a stumbled jog, circling around the wreckage. Jelica was on her knees. She looked up, gave him a brief smile.

He ran to her side, dropped to his knees, and wrapped his left arm around her. "How did you do that?"

I… I don't know.

"Are you okay?"

All I know is there's a price to pay… a balancing in the universe.

Jelica's eyes rolled and then she began to wobble as if lightheaded. She clung to him to steady herself and he let out an audible cry.

You're hurt.

"It's nothing. Are you okay?"

I'll live.

"Miguel… is he… did he make it out?" Tears coursed down his cheeks as he stared at the ruins around them.

I can't hear him. She shook her head solemnly. *But that doesn't mean anything. That doesn't mean there's not a chance.* Jelica gasped and stiffened against him. *Jesus… when will it end?*

"What?" Conner turned to see humanlike forms lurking in billowing ash. The shapes multiplied as they came closer to them. He saw so many familiar faces as they emerged from the shadows: Uncle, Mr. Entrican, Bonita Ramos, so many others.

"Can you stand?"

I can't move. All my strength is gone.

Conner tried to lift her from the ground, but he was too weakened and injured by their ordeal. He sighed and tried again, but it was pointless.

Conner, you have to go.

"I can't leave you. Not again. I can't... I can't carry you with this ruined arm. I'm staying."

Do you want to save me? Do you want to end this?

"Of course I do. But what the hell am I supposed to do?"

Use that. Jelica pointed to Conner's backpack. *I lifted a building off of you with my mind. I'm no different than you.*

"But—"

It's our only chance. I'll be fine. I'll hold them off. She grinned, but it wasn't real, not even close. *Trust me.*

Conner looked from the backpack, to the unclean spirits closing in, to Jelica's face. She looked so incredibly tired, but also resigned, and somehow, at peace.

Go...

"When this is over, we're going to have a long talk." Conner leaned in, kissed the top of her head. He continued: *And then, I'm never going to let you go.*

I wouldn't have it any other way.

Conner hooked his left arm through the pack's strap and took off for the nearest cinderblock wall. If what Jelica had said was true, he could think of only one thing that could possibly save them.

He glanced back and saw the circle of spirits closing in around Jelica.

Jinny, her black bloated tongue jutting from her cracked lips, groaned. "You took my home away from me. You slept in my bed, you whore..."

He felt a surge of panic and wanted to kick himself for leaving her.

Jinny, his neighbor who'd overdosed on Christmas day all those years ago, cast an accusatory finger at Jelica. "You and your whore mother, your whore sister—"

Suddenly, the air around Jelica seemed to vibrate, and then an explosion of silvery light burst from where she stood. Conner closed his eyes at the painful brightness. When he opened them again, the spirits had gone and Jelica was on her hands and knees, panting from the exertion.

She lifted her head and gave him a slight nod. *Do it.*

He took off at a trot, hoping that somehow this night would come to an end. One way or another, it had to end.

Ten

Conner stopped in front of the nearest expanse of cinderblocks and dropped his pack. He instinctively reached with his right arm to unzip it, and the shooting pain in his shoulder nearly staggered him. He breathed through the waves of agony until it calmed down, then managed to open the zipper with his left hand.

He pried off the lids of all the cartons of chalk and dumped them at his feet. The wall was relatively clean, a pale white canvas of fairly new paint with evident hints of something obscene buried beneath.

"Well, Jelica, I hope you're right…" he whispered and picked up a dark gray chalk.

As he always did before starting a new panel of his comic, he closed his eyes and visualized his subject. Every detail came into fine focus. The image was so clear and believable in his mind's eye that he could smell its musky sent, could hear its horrible throaty growl in his ears.

He opened his eyes, and the wall became an empty three-dimensional void which presented an infinite number of possibilities. He set to it, his left hand transferring the image from his mind to the blank wall. He couldn't see the image as a whole from his close vantage, but as he took up one chalk after another, feathering texture and nuance, mixing colors and adding depth, he could feel it come alive, just as every work of art did under the intense scrutiny of its creator.

The world around him pulled away, all but the heat of the sun warming his back as the day took hold.

As if guided by some unseen hand, the chalks scratched the rough block wall, adding flourishes and gouges as the final details took shape. He needed more browns, more blacks, more reds for the eyes. He pressed so hard to bring the image to life that the chalk rubbed away to nothing and he was soon scraping his fingers into the wall. He abraded his skin until his blood soon commingled with the chalk in a sticky paste.

The sound of a screen door screeching open and slamming shut drew his attention. Conner whipped around on his heel.

How did I not notice…?

Jerry, his stepdad, a man long dead, and thankfully so, stepped down from the burned ruined of the trailer they'd once shared. He tugged on his tangled beard, forever stained below his bottom lip with tobacco spit. He wore filthy jeans that sagged below his hip bones and a white tank top, soiled at the pits. His left arm flexed as he pulled at his beard, the tattoo on the forearm becoming visible. It was unreadable from this distance, but Conner knew the words well—*Blood and Soil.*

"What are you doing waking me up, boy?" Jerry cleared his throat and spit.

"You're dead."

"You always had a way of stating the obvious. '*You're hurting me, Jerry. I won't tell anyone. Promise.*' Gab-gab-gab, cry-cry-cry. Such a pussy."

Conner flashed to a long-buried memory of Jerry looming above him as he removed his belt and doubled it over before snapping it menacingly like a firecracker. Jerry, reaching for him. Jerry coming for him, coming to steal his innocence.

"You're not real."

"Wanna bet I can prove different?"

Jerry sauntered closer, chuckling. He scratched at his balls, then cracked his knuckles—each action, each minute detail so precisely *Jerry* that Conner felt thrown back in time. "I should've smothered you like an unwanted kitten when I had the chance. I came close so many times, but your momma always managed to talk me out of it. She weren't nothing to look at, but her dick sucking skills were next level." Again, the chuckling.

Conner felt small, twelve years old again and helpless. He backed away until the wall stopped him. He was trapped, paralyzed.

"Now, you, on the other hand, was always something pretty to look at." Jerry closed to ten feet. Five.

"Jer?" a voice called out from the burnt husk of their trailer. "Jer-bear, you coming back to bed, or what?"

Jerry chuckled, reached out, traced the curve of Conner's chin. Conner shuddered, nearly vomited.

"You know, your momma was a dirty, broken hag long before I ever met her. But I don't need to go back to her. No, sir. Not with you coming back to the 'Pines. I could just make you mine, see if those skills your momma's got in great supply got passed down."

"No… stop." Conner cringed, closed his eyes, wanting nothing more than this nightmare to end.

Jerry ran his thumb across Conner's lips, and Conner couldn't shirk the flood of memory the illicit touch awakened in him. He pressed himself flat against the wall, his palms slapping the chalk mural at his back.

"I said stop it!" His bloody hand tingled as if electricity flowed from his fingertips.

At first he only felt Jerry's sour whiskey breath against his face. But then hot panting breath buffeted the back of his nape, breath rank with desperation and laden with the stomach-turning odor of spoiled steak.

It worked. My God, it worked.

A rising, horrible growl vibrated against Conner's shoulder blades. And just shy of an outright howl, something from behind knocked him flat to the ground.

An alpha werewolf, more vicious than he ever managed to render for his comic, took one stride on all fours before springing at Jerry, knocking him to the blackened earth. Jerry tried to kick away from it, to crab-walk backward, but it was no use.

"No-no-no…" his step-father said. "It doesn't have to be this way."

"Yeah, Jerry, I think it does." Conner got to his feet and dusted himself off.

The werewolf stood a head taller than either Jerry or Conner. Despite being covered in thick gray and brown fur, its muscles rippled visibly in its haunches, its broad back. It tilted its head back and let loose with a blood-curdling howl.

Jerry tried getting to his feet, but the werewolf swiped its claws across his chest, carving deep bloody furrows into his flesh.

Jerry cried out in agony, unable to defend himself. The werewolf advanced, pinning Jerry's shoulders to the ground. It leaned in close and sniffed as drool dripped in slimy bands from its chin. And then it lunged, burying its teeth in his neck. Jerry's cries quickly stuttered to a gurgling end. The hot blood on its lips seemed to spur it to frenzy, and it continued to slash and gnash at his neck and torso until the clean white of his spine was showing.

"Jer-bear… what's going on out there?" Conner's mom said from within the ruins of the trailer. The conflagration had destroyed the roof and shattered the windows. Nothing could be living within.

The sound of his mom's voice after all these years struck Conner like a physical blow. He felt like the wind had been knocked out of him as long buried emotions continued to bubble to the surface.

"Jer-bear, come on back in here. You still got that half a rock you promised to share with me…"

Once again the screen door opened with a screech before slamming shut. Conner couldn't look. Seeing her would only lead to madness. Her bare feet crunched spent cinders.

"Connie… is that you? My baby boy?"

The sound of a revving engine drew Conner's attention. He turned quickly, saw Miguel leaning out from a rusted and fire-scorched pick-up truck. "Get outta the way, pendejo!"

The truck's knobby tires kicked up sprays of blackened gravel. Its front bumper had been modified with a snow plow's blade. Corrugated metal covered its windows like battle armor.

It closed on Conner, and beyond, the spirit of Conner's dead mother.

Conner leapt out of the way, and the truck passed him in a blur. Conner heard the impact of the phantom body colliding with the plow blade, and then the violent upheaval of the truck slamming into the remains of the trailer.

Conner staggered to his feet, his shoulder screaming in pain no matter how he tried to brace it against his body. He trotted over to the truck just as the driver's side door opened.

Miguel climbed out of the truck and shook his head, momentarily dazed. When he saw Conner he smiled, and he suddenly looked twenty years younger.

"What did you do?" Conner asked.

"Easy there. Hold on, hold on." Miguel looked at Conner's condition with concern. "Please tell me I didn't do that to you."

"No, it wasn't you—"

"Jesus, what's that?"

Conner looked to where he was pointing. The werewolf had its maw buried deep in the remains of Jerry's belly. Its red eyes gleamed at them from above the wound.

"Uh… yeah, that's all me. I totally own that… but even so, I think we better get out of here before it turns on us."

"Let's get Jelica," Miguel said. "Where is she?"

"Back…" Conner said, pausing as he pointed in the direction of the laundromat. "I left her back there."

The glow of stoked flames lit the top of the slight rise leading to the laundromat at the front of the trailer park.

"What's going on?" Miguel asked.

Conner said nothing, but took off toward the laundromat. Even with dawn taking full hold, the light from a fire blazed brighter. Conner had the worst scenarios flitting through his brain as they neared the final approach.

Miguel ran ahead and picked up a discarded backpack. "Empty. It was Jelica's."

"What was inside?"

"She never said." Miguel took off again, and Conner followed. "Jesus, why didn't we demand to know? What did she do, Bro? What did she do?"

They rounded the corner and Miguel nearly tripped over a gasoline can. Footprints led away from it, footprints outlined in low orange flames.

At the light post, under the glow of the lone street light spared from the children of Sunny Pines and untouched by the destructive force of the fire, Jelica stood with her arms spread wide. The unclean spirits of Sunny Pines gathered around her, drew closer, like moths to open flame. One after another, the spirits reached out, and when their ethereal fingertips touched the flame, they turned to sooty ash. One after another after another.

"Jelica! No!" Conner moved to try to save her, but Miguel wrapped his arms around him. Conner struggled to get away, but Miguel held him fast.

I'm sorry, Conner. I truly am. Her blue eyes found theirs. She looked so at peace.

Conner couldn't help it; he was now openly sobbing. "Why are you doing this?"

I needed you both to return. I couldn't end this without all three of us present. I tried by myself… with the fire, but it didn't help. It only made things worse.

"You used us."

I'm sorry. I tried to find some other way, but I wasn't strong enough.

"Jelica… I love you. I've always loved you."

I always loved you, too.

The sooty ash quickly piled up until it completely blanketed Jelica, until it smothered the flames engulfing her.

"Jelica..."

Miguel let go of Conner. As they both slowly approached the pile of ash, a wind kicked up and battered the mound, eroding it little by little until nothing remained.

$\mathcal{E}leven$

Conner had two surgeries to repair his shoulder. Despite coming through the repairs and physical therapy as near to normal as possible, he never managed to return to his previous form artistically. Not even close. He could draw basic figures, but any genius within the work was no longer present. No longer able to make his living through his art, he sold the rights to his werewolf comic for a substantial chunk of money and retired young. He spent most of his free time scouring ever-more obscure news sources, searching for some clue to explain what had happened at Sunny Pines.

He never talked to Miguel after his second surgery on his shoulder, even though they'd promised to stay in touch. If Conner were to hazard a guess, he figured Miguel would still be able to manage the basics of auto mechanics, but his otherworldly skills were most likely extinguished as well.

When Miguel and Conner were discovered stumbling away from Sunny Pines, their injuries were attributed to their foolish decision to explore the burned remains of their childhood neighborhood. No evidence of their final night inside the 'Pines had ever surfaced. No bones, no blood, no werewolf hair. And even after the land was razed and construction began on the apartment buildings that would fill the area, no trace of Jelica had ever surfaced, either.

Sunny Pines

When the Sunny Pines apartment towers opened, Conner walked the well-lit sidewalks at night, searching for any trace of Jelica… and reluctantly, any other spirit that might still linger there.